The Mustang

Rachel Damon Criscione

The Rosen Publishing Group's

PowerKids Press™

New York

To Honey Zweifach, a good friend and a most admirable woman

Published in 2007 by The Rosen Publishing Group, Inc.
29 East 21st Street, New York, NY 10010

First Edition

Editors: Melissa Acevedo and Amelie von Zumbusch
Book Design: Ginny Chu

Photo Credits: Cover, title page © Momatiuk Eastcott/Animals Animals; pp. 4, 15, 16, 19 © Bob Langrish; p. 7 © Bettmann/Corbis; pp. 8, 11 Library of Congress Prints and Photographs Division; p. 12 Nevada Historical Society; p. 20 Photo and pedigree courtesy of Vickie Ives, Karma Farms.

Acknowledgment: A special thanks to Alicia Recor and her horse Sahib.

Library of Congress Cataloging-in-Publication Data

Criscione, Rachel Damon.
  The Mustang / Rachel Damon Criscione.— 1st ed.
      p. cm. — (The Library of horses)
  Includes bibliographical references and index.
  ISBN 1-4042-3452-7 (lib. bdg.)
  1. Mustang—Juvenile literature. 2. Wild horses—West (U.S.)—Juvenile literature. I. Title.

SF293.M9C75 2007
599.665'5—dc22

                                                                   2005029479

Manufactured in the United States of America

Table of Contents

Mustangs are very sure footed. This means that they can run or walk over uneven ground without tripping or falling.

Mustangs in the American West

Mustangs have captured the imaginations of horse lovers around the world. These beautiful wild horses have been wandering the plains and mountains of the United States for centuries. Wild mustangs have no owners to feed them or provide housing for them. They care for themselves and are not easily **tamed** or caught.

At first farmers and **ranchers** in the West did not like mustangs because the horses would drift onto private property. However, in time, many people grew to respect these creatures for their strength and independence. Mustangs are so important to Americans that the government decided to **protect** these creatures. The **Bureau** of Land Management and the United States Forest Service now oversees and protects these animals.

Spanish Horses

Wild horses lived in North America thousands and thousands of years ago. However, they died out around 8000 B.C. Spanish **explorers** brought horses back to the New World in the 1500s. Queen Isabella of Spain sent the explorers to claim what is now known as North America and South America for her country.

The Spanish horses were small, strong animals. Even though they were strong, sometimes only half of them were able to live through the long journey across the Atlantic Ocean. The Spanish used some of the horses that reached the New World to work on ranches, or large farms for raising cattle, horses, or sheep. At some point the horses either escaped from the Spanish settlers or were turned loose by their owners. The Spanish horses **bred** in the wild and formed herds. They spread upward from Mexico into the United States and the western plains country.

This drawing shows Spanish explorers and their horses searching for gold in Texas in 1540.

Horses became important to many Native American peoples. Some Native Americans even measured wealth by the number of horses a person owned.

Native Americans

When Native Americans living in North America first saw men on horses, they were afraid. They thought the horse and the rider were one animal. They soon realized that this was not the case. They also discovered how useful horses could be.

Spanish horses changed the Native Americans' way of life. They now had more freedom to move about and hunt. A nation that had horses was considered more powerful than one that did not own any. Sometimes horses escaped and formed herds that ran wild. Some of these horses went north to the Great Plains of the American West. These horses were called mustangs. Their name comes from the Spanish word *mesteño*, which means "strayed" or "wild."

Mustangers

Once free and wandering the Americas, mustangs began to breed. By the 1800s, there were millions of mustangs living in the western grasslands from Mexico to Canada, west of the Mississippi River. There were so many mustangs that farmers began to object to their taking up so much land. Farmers and ranchers began to think of the mustangs as pests.

The United States Department of the Interior's Bureau of Land Management permitted people to kill some of the mustangs. They thought this was a way to make the herds of mustangs smaller. The people who hunted these horses were called mustangers. Mustangers often chased the horses with guns, dogs, and planes until the tired mustangs dropped dead.

This picture from 1835 shows mustangers trying to capture wild horses.

Velma Johnston, shown here, grew up in Nevada. She helped found several wild-horse refuges in her home state. The refuges are safe places where the horses can wander free.

Wild Horse Annie

In 1950, Velma Johnston, a horse lover, found out what mustangers were doing and decided to try to save the wild horses. Johnston, who later became known as Wild Horse Annie, started talking to reporters about how the mustangs were being treated. Then she asked children to write letters to **Congress** asking to save the mustangs.

In 1959, thanks to Johnston's efforts, the Wild Horse Annie Act was passed. It said using planes to hunt horses was illegal. Johnston was not satisfied, and she continued fighting. In 1971, Congress passed the Wild Free-Roaming Horse and Burro Act. This law gave the U.S. government power to protect and control wild horses and burros, or donkeys, on the nation's public rangelands. After more than 20 years of hard work, Johnston had helped to save the mustangs!

A Different Kind of Horse

The mustang is a mix of different **breeds**. This is why every mustang is different. They come in many colors, sizes, and shapes. Mustangs are small compared to other horses. Mustangs are usually between 13 and 16 hands tall. A hand is 4 inches (10 cm) long. All horses are measured in hands. They are measured from the ground to the high point between their shoulders, called the withers. Mustangs weigh from 700 to 1,000 pounds (318–454 kg). They have short legs and backs, but they are very strong.

Mustangs have excellent eyesight. This helps protect them in the wild. Their eyes can move independently of each other. That means they can look forward with one eye and behind them with the other!

Mustangs can have many different colors or markings. This mustang is dun colored. Dun horses are light brown with black manes and black tails.

This mustang is wearing a Western saddle. A saddle is the seat that carries the rider on a horse's back. Western saddles are larger and heavier than other saddles are.

Mustang Uses

Mustangs are not used to being around people. It is therefore hard to own a mustang. They are used to wandering free. Mustangs must be carefully trained before a person can ride them. However, mustangs are true and useful horses once a person has earned their trust.

Mustangs are smart and quick and have won events in barrel racing and **endurance** riding. Tamed mustangs make great trail horses because they are strong and know how to watch where they put their feet. The **Pony Express** and the United States **Cavalry** once used these horses.

Every year there is a National Wild Horse and Burro Show. Well-trained mustangs and their owners enter all kinds of Western events. Prizes are given to the winners of each event.

Special Training

Mustangs live in the wild and other animals consider them **prey**. This is why mustangs will run away from anything that comes near them. You can train a wild horse to trust you, but it may take a long time.

Mustangs have to get used to being around people. Owners need to make sure that a mustang trusts them before they attempt to ride it. Mustangs have to be trained to wear a saddle. The trainer will start by rubbing the horse's back and shoulders with a cloth. Then the trainer places the cloth on the horse's back. Gradually he will add more and more cloths. When the mustang is ready, the trainer will place a saddle on the horse's back.

Mustangs need to be trained to wear a bridle. A bridle is the set of bands that fits over a horse's head.

This is a pedigree of Rowdy Yates, a Spanish Colonial Mustang. Pedigrees trace the history and bloodlines of an individual horse. The picture to the right shows Rowdy Yates.

				Book Cliff Mtns, Utah
			Book Cliff Mtns, Utah stallion	Book Cliff Mtns, Utah
		Narragansett		Book Cliff Mtns, Utah
	Grandsire	SMR-285	Book Cliff Mtns, Utah Mare	
Sire: Jack Slade **				Book Cliff Mtns, Utah
Reg.# SMR-668				
			Jack SMR-59	Book Cliff Mtns, Utah
		Sooner		Book Cliff Mtns, Utah
	Grand-dam	SMR-166		Buckshot SMR-1
			Shoshoni SMR-75	Teton SMR-24

Name: Rowdy Yates * ^^ ** /+ //
HOA-1008; SMR-1407;
AIHR O-1344; SSMA-921

				Sulphur Mtns, Utah
			Sulphur Mtns., Utah Stallion	Sulphur Mtns, Utah
		Doby		Sulphur Mtns, Utah
	Grandsire	SMR-406	Sulphur Mtns., Utah Mare	
Dam: Esperanza ***				Sulphur Mtns, Utah
Reg.# HOA-1025; SMR-640; SSMA-535				
			Book Cliff Mtns, Utah stallion	Book Cliff Mtns, Utah
		Blue Corn		Book Cliff Mtns, Utah
	Grand-dam	SMR-138		Book Cliff Mtns, Utah
		SSMA-531	Book Cliff Mtns, Utah mare	Book Cliff Mtns, Utah

- SMR Grande Conquistador Award; ** Sire of Champions; *** Dam of Champions
- ^^ AIHR Hall of Fame Award; ^^^ AIHR Supreme Hall of Fame;
  /+ AIHR National Show Champion; // NATRC Trail Champion

The Spanish Mustang

Mustangs started out as pure Spanish horses, but over time they mixed with other breeds. In the 1950s, a rancher named Robert Brislawn worried that the original Spanish mustangs were dying out. Brislawn chose Native American horses and wild mustangs whose ancestors were almost all Spanish horses to form his own herd. He used this herd to breed more horses like the original Spanish mustangs.

In 1957, Brislawn founded the Spanish Mustang **Registry**. To be listed in the registry, almost all a horse's ancestors must be Spanish horses. Some Spanish Mustangs come from carefully bred herds, like the one on Brislawn's Cayuse Ranch. Others come from wild herds, such as the Sulphur Herd in Utah's Needle Mountain Range.

Adopting Mustangs

Today more than 30,000 wild mustangs live on government land. The Department of the Interior's Bureau of Land Management keeps mustangs from becoming a problem for farmers and ranchers. They do this by capturing thousands of the horses each year and allowing the public to **adopt** them. Between 1973 and 2000, more than 178,000 wild horses and burros have been adopted throughout the United States.

Each year the Department of the Interior gathers extra horses from land where there are too many horses. These horses are put up for adoption. People who adopt a mustang pay about $125 and promise to take good care of the animal for one year. If the horse's new owner can prove that the horse has received proper care and treatment during that year, the horse becomes officially his or hers.

Glossary

adopt (uh-DOPT) To take something for your own or as your own choice.

bred (BRED) Made babies.

breeds (BREEDZ) Groups of animals that look alike and have the same relatives.

bureau (BYUR-oh) A branch of business or government that specializes in a
  certain thing.

cavalry (KA-vul-ree) The part of an army that rides and fights on horseback.

Congress (KON-gres) The part of the U.S. government that makes laws.

endurance (en-DUR-ints) Strength and the ability to go long distances without
  getting tired easily.

explorers (ek-SPLOR-urz) People who travel and look for new land.

Pony Express (POH-nee ik-SPRES) A system during 1860-1861 that delivered letters across
  the western United States by riders on fast horses.

prey (PRAY) An animal that is hunted by another animal for food.

protect (pruh-TEKT) To keep from harm.

ranchers (RAN-cherz) People who have large farms for raising cattle, horses, or sheep.

registry (REH-jih-stree) An official record book or group.

tamed (TAYMD) Made a wild thing gentle.

Index

Web Sites

Due to the changing nature of Internet links, PowerKids Press has developed an online list of Web sites related to the subject of this book. This site is updated regularly. Please use this link to access the list:

www.powerkidslinks.com/horse/mustang/